Patsy the Pussycat

by Mabel Watts
illustrated by Terri Super

A GOLDEN BOOK • NEW YORK
Western Publishing Company, Inc., Racine, Wisconsin 53404

 Library of Congress Catalog Card Number: 85-82186 ISBN 0-307-07015-8
MCMXCIII

Patsy the pussycat thought Farmer John's kitchen was the nicest place in the whole wide world.

There was a saucer of cream to drink.

And a dish of food to eat.

And a little catnip mouse to toss and catch.

And a soft pillow for Patsy to sleep on.

All day long the kitchen kettle sang with a hum-hum. The kitchen clock said tick-tock. And, all day long, Patsy purred.

Patsy was a happy cat.

Until one morning... the kettle did not sing. The clock did not tick-tock. And Patsy did not purr.

She did not purr because her saucer of cream was gone.

So was her dish of food.

So was her catnip mouse.

So was her soft pillow.

Such a morning! Everything in Farmer John's kitchen was upside down. Everywhere there was hustle and bustle and noise. Farmer John's wife, Rebecca, was painting the kitchen—PATSY'S kitchen!

“Stop it!” Patsy meowed. “Stop it, I say!”
But things went right on going on…
Swish, boom, bang, slap!
“Meow!” said Patsy. “This is no place for me!”

Up went her nose. Up went her tail.
Pit-a-pat...pit-a-pat...

Patsy went out into the yard to tell her troubles to Digger the dog.

"Don't worry," said Digger. "You can help me bury my bones. You can help me dig them up again, too. I'll even let you sleep with me in my doghouse."

Patsy turned up her whiskers.

"No, thank you," she sniffed. "Your doghouse doesn't look big enough for both of us. Besides, I don't think I want your old doggy bones. But thanks a lot."

Pit-a-pat . . . pit-a-pat . . .

Patsy went into the barn and told her troubles to Henry the horse.

"Cheer up!" said Henry. "You can help me pull the wagon for Farmer John. You can eat my oats, and at night you can sleep on my straw bed with me. Won't that be fun!"

"Not for me!" said Patsy. "I'm much too small to pull a wagon. And I don't think I want to eat oats or sleep on a straw bed, either. But thanks just the same."

Pit-a-pat... pit-a-pat...

Soon Patsy was in the meadow telling her troubles to Carrie the cow.

"Stay with me," said Carrie. "There is plenty of good clover to eat here and lots of soft grass to lie on. There are birds and bees and buttercups, too."

"I like birds and bees and buttercups," said Patsy. "But I don't eat clover. And I want my own pillow to lie on."

Pit-a-pat . . . pit-a-pat . . .

Patsy went in the henhouse and told her troubles to Hilda the hen.

"Cut-cut-cut!" cackled Hilda. "Thank goodness you were clever enough to come to me with your troubles! Live with me, and you can peck for corn and scratch for worms. At night you can perch on my roost with me."

"No," said Patsy. "I could never peck for corn, or scratch for worms, or perch on a chicken roost at night—because, you see, I am a cat!"

Pit-a-pat . . . pit-a-pat . . .

Patsy went in the pigpen and told her troubles to Pinky the pig.

"You can move in with me," grunted Pinky. "Here you will get all the mash you can eat, and my pen is cozy to sleep in. And we can play together in my squishy-squashy mud. Think of that!"

Patsy looked at the mash. She looked at the pigpen. She looked at the squishy-squashy mud. "Thanks for the invitation," said Patsy. "But I can't eat mash. And I don't like mud!"

Pit-a-pat . . . pit-a-pat . . .

Patsy went out in the woods and told her troubles to Bingo the bunny.

"Dear, dear!" said Bingo. "Things can't be as bad as all that!"

"Oh, but they *are*," meowed Patsy.

"Then you stay with me," said Bingo. "Here in the woods we live like one big happy family. At work, or at play. Every night we hippety-hop out in the moonlight. Then we scoot down into our warm little burrows to sleep!"

"Burrows are only big enough for bunnies," said Patsy. "I am a cat. And I live with people. Thanks just the same."

Patsy sat down to rest. She washed her paw and thought about all her animal friends. How kind they had been to her. They had all wanted to help. But Patsy knew there was only one place she could ever be happy. So...

Pit-a-pat . . . pit-a-pat . . .

Back she went to Farmer John's kitchen.
There was Patsy's saucer of cream.
There was her dish of food.
There was her little catnip mouse.
There was her soft pillow, too.

Hum-hum sang the kettle. Tick-tock said the clock.

Everything was right side up in Farmer John's kitchen once again.

"Here, kitty," called the farmer's wife, Rebecca.

Patsy purred. She was back where she belonged. And she was the happiest pussycat in the whole wide world.